Mud Puddle

Story by Robert Munsch
Illustrations by Sami Suomalainen

Annick Press
Toronto • New York

Second printing, revised edition, February 1998

Annick Press gratefully acknowledges the support of the
Canada Council and the Ontario Arts Council.

Cataloguing in Publication Data
  Munsch, Robert N., 1945 -
    Mud puddle

(Munsch for kids)
Rev. ed.
ISBN 1-55037-469-9 (bound) ISBN 1-55037-468-0 (pbk.)

I. Suomalainen, Sami. II. Title. III. Series: Munsch, Robert N., 1945-
Munsch for kids.

PS8576.U575M8 1995   jC813'.54   C95-931712-0
PZ7.M85Mu 1995

Distributed in Canada by:
Firefly Books Ltd.
3680 Victoria Park Avenue
Willowdale, ON
M2H 3K1

Published in the U.S.A. by Annick Press (U.S.) Ltd.
Distributed in the U.S.A. by:
Firefly Books (U.S.) Inc.
P.O. Box 1338
Ellicott Station
Buffalo, NY 14205

Printed and bound in Canada by
Metropole Litho, Québec

To Jeffrey—R.M.

To my wife, June—S.S.

Jule Ann's mother bought her clean new clothes.

Jule Ann put on a clean new shirt and buttoned it up the front. She put on clean new pants and buttoned them up the front. Then she walked outside and sat down under the apple tree.

Unfortunately, hiding up in the
apple tree, there was a mud puddle.
It saw Jule Ann sitting there and it
jumped right on her head.

She got completely all over muddy.
Even her ears were full of mud.

Jule Ann ran inside yelling, "Mummy, Mummy! A Mud Puddle jumped on me."

Her mother picked her up, took off all her clothes and dropped her into a tub of water. She scrubbed Jule Ann till she was red all over.

She washed out her ears.

She washed out her eyes.

She even washed out her mouth.

Jule Ann put on a clean new shirt and buttoned it up the front. She put on clean new pants and buttoned them up the front. Then she looked out the back door. She couldn't see a mud puddle anywhere, so she walked outside and sat down in her sand box.

The sand box was next to the house and hiding up on top of the house there was a mud puddle.

It saw Jule Ann sitting down
there and it jumped right on her
head. She got completely all over
muddy. Even her nose was full
of mud.

Jule Ann ran inside yelling,
"Mummy, Mummy! A Mud
Puddle jumped on me."

Jule Ann's mother picked her
up, took off all her clothes and
dropped her into a tub of water.
She scrubbed Jule Ann till she
was red all over.

She washed out her ears.
She washed out her eyes.
She washed out her mouth.
She even washed out her nose.

Jule Ann put on a clean new shirt and buttoned it up the front. Then she put on clean new pants and buttoned them up the front. Then she had an idea. She reached way back in the closet and got a big yellow raincoat. She put it on and walked outside. There was no mud puddle anywhere, so she yelled, "Hey, Mud Puddle!"

Nothing happened, so she yelled, even louder, "Hey, Mud Puddle!!"

Jule Ann was standing in the sunshine in her raincoat, getting very hot. She pulled back her hood.

Nothing happened. She took off her raincoat.

As soon as she took off her coat, out from behind the dog house, there came the mud puddle.

It ran across the grass and jumped right on Jule Ann's head.

She got completely all over muddy. Jule Ann ran inside yelling, "Mummy, Mummy! A Mud Puddle jumped on me."

Her mother picked her up, took off all her clothes and dropped her into a tub full of water. She scrubbed Jule Ann till she was red all over.

She washed out her ears.
She washed out her eyes.
She washed out her mouth.
She washed out her nose.
She even washed out her belly button.

Jule Ann put on a clean new shirt and buttoned it up the front. She put on clean new pants and buttoned them up the front. Then she sat beside the back door because she was afraid to go outside.

Then she had an idea.

She reached up to the sink and took a bar of smelly yellow soap. She gave it a smell – yecch! She took another bar of smelly yellow soap and gave it a smell – yecch! She put the smelly yellow soap in her pockets. Then she ran out into the middle of the back yard and yelled, "Hey, Mud Puddle!"

The mud puddle jumped over the fence and ran right toward her.

Jule Ann threw a bar of soap right into the mud puddle's middle. The mud puddle stopped.

Jule Ann threw the other bar of soap right into the mud puddle. The mud puddle said, "Awk, yecch, wackh!"

It ran across the grass, jumped over the fence, and never came back.

Other books in the Munsch for Kids series: